DATE DUE

FEB 0 2005			
FEB 1 2005			

THE GIRL
on the HIGH-DIVING
HORSE

For Ted Lewin, who remembers the best Atlantic City, and for
Arnette French, a diving-horse girl whose memory lives on.

—LOH

In memory of my mother and father and my father's parents,
who all loved Atlantic City.

–TL

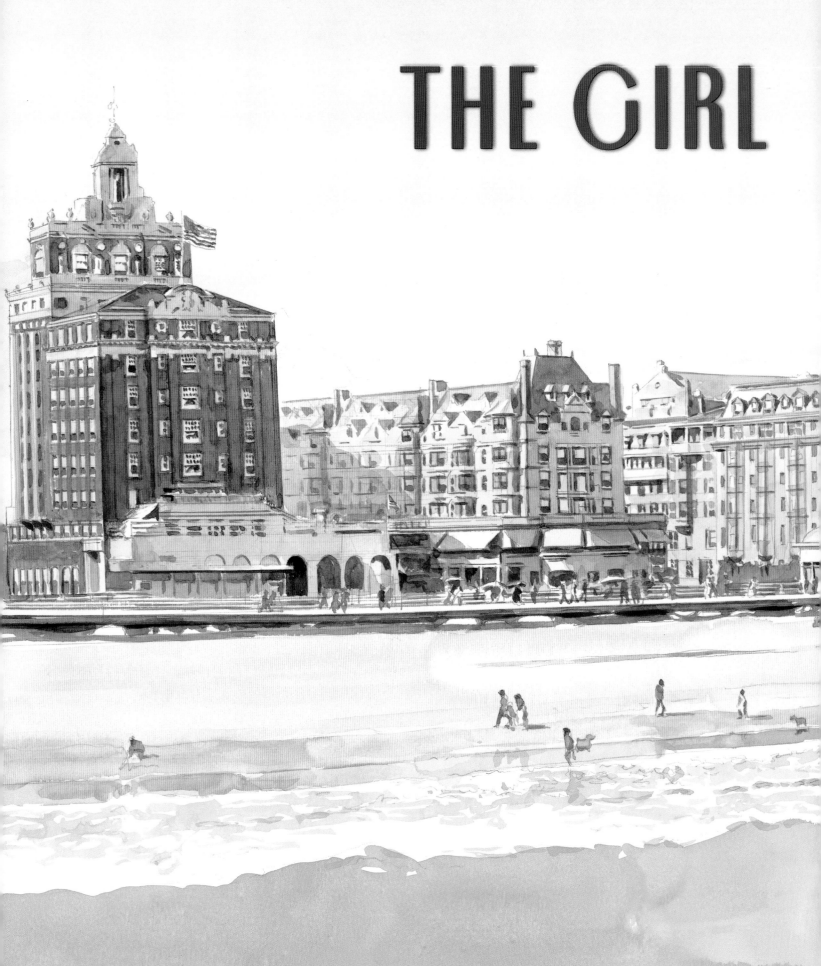

THE GIRL

on the HIGH-DIVING HORSE

by Linda Oatman High

illustrated by Ted Lewin

Philomel Books

Sea breeze tickles my eyes
as Papa and I lug our trunks
and Papa's photography equipment
across the boardwalk.
It's the summer of 1936,
and Papa's job is to take
lots of pictures of
Atlantic City.

As we walk, I can't help but gawk
at boxing kangaroos, card-playing cats,
and a dog on a surfboard. I stare at
daredevils sitting on flagpoles,
boardwalk bands
and dancing tigers,
fantastic sand artists
and human cannonballs.
This is a wondrous land
of sand and stunts and fun,
and I feel so lucky to be
staying all summer long!

"Our hotel home," says Papa,
stopping at a castle-shaped place
rising pink and high as a sunrise
into blue New Jersey sky.

Papa and I drop off cumbersome
luggage, then ride the rolling chair
to the Steel Pier, where Papa says
the high-diving horse show is going on.

I can't believe my eyes when
an enormous white horse sprints fast
up a steep slanting ramp, hooves
hammering and his flashing dark eyes
sparking stars of fire.
"That's Red Lips," Papa whispers.
"He's going to dive."
A pretty teenaged girl, wearing
a blue bathing suit with a leather helmet
perched on her curls, climbs a ladder,
and Papa claps. "That's the girl
on the high-diving horse," he explains.
"She's crazy-brave." The girl waves,
and when the horse storms snorting
onto the platform, she leaps upon his back.

The crowd is still, holding its breath.
The horse pauses for a moment,
tilting down,
head bent
toward the tank of water below.
His mane blows in the wind,
his hooves slide a bit,
and then he jumps,
diving.
It's like flying: the horse and rider
suspended high
in silent air . . .
dropping.

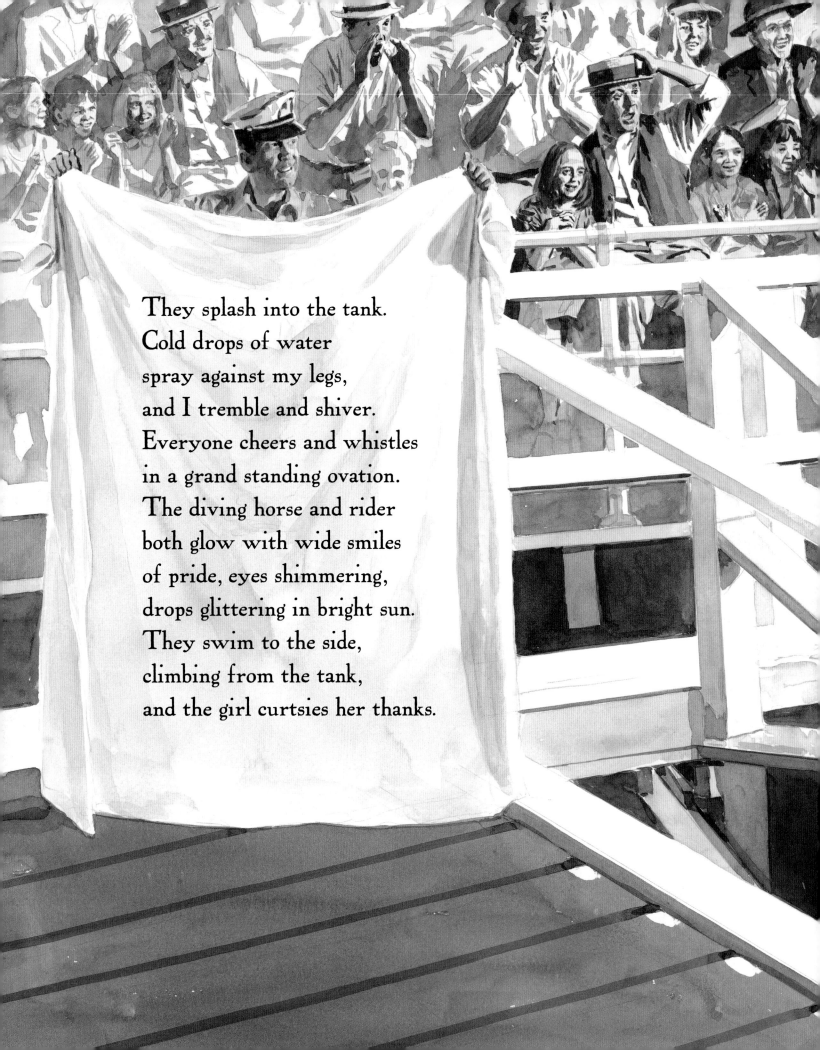

They splash into the tank.
Cold drops of water
spray against my legs,
and I tremble and shiver.
Everyone cheers and whistles
in a grand standing ovation.
The diving horse and rider
both glow with wide smiles
of pride, eyes shimmering,
drops glittering in bright sun.
They swim to the side,
climbing from the tank,
and the girl curtsies her thanks.

I close my eyes, picturing myself
as the girl on the high-diving horse.
But of course, I know
that Papa would be too afraid
to let me attempt a stunt
so crazy and brave. Every day,
as Papa works, I ride the rolling chair
alone to the Steel Pier. I watch
the show over and over, dreaming
each time of being
the girl on the high-diving horse.

One day, Papa comes along
to the Steel Pier, taking photos
of the high-diving horse show.
We go to the stables afterward,
clicking pictures of magnificent
horses in their stalls. I help Papa
to take pictures of two sisters—
Arnette and Sonora: famous girls
on the high-diving horses.
Then, Papa snaps his camera,
taking pictures of me feeding carrots
and apples to Red Lips. I kiss
the big horse on his velvet-soft nose.

"How would you like to sit
on his back?" whispers Sonora,
lifting me up onto the horse.
Towering over Papa, head against
the clouds, I feel as if I could
ride to the top of the world. If only
I could be a diving-horse girl!
Every day, I go to the stables,
making friends with the horses.
Arnette and Sonora allow me
to feed and water and lead
and brush, and I fall in love
with each and every one of the
high-diving horses. I bring
brown sugar for treats, feeding
each horse from the palm
of my hand. I make a braid
of hair from their manes,
placing it beneath my pillow
so that when I sleep,
I dream of the horses.

Summertime gallops by, and
at the end of August, I'm feeling
like I could just cry and cry.
I don't want to leave the diving horses,
not ever, and I wish to stay here
forever. "But Ivy Cordelia," says Papa,
"we need to go home to Philadelphia."
I hate the sound of the train at night,
and the thought of leaving the horses
behind. In the purple-early morning
of our last day of summer,
Papa and I ride the rolling chair,
first to the ocean for one last dip,
and then to the Steel Pier.

Seagulls squawk and the ocean rolls
as I sulk and mope, holding
the horsehair braid close to my heart.
Parting with the horses
is the hardest thing I've ever
had to do. Sad and blue,
I can't even look the sisters
in their eyes when I tell them good-bye.

"Ivy," says Arnette,
"I have a surprise."
Arnette puts a leather helmet
upon my head, then lifts me up
onto Red Lips. She winks
at Papa, who smiles.

"Ready to dive?" she asks,
and I catch my breath.
Heart pounding like hooves, I nod,
and Arnette leads Red Lips to the ramp.
She leaps up, sitting in front of me.
"Hold tight," she says. "We're going
to fly." My eyes open wide
as Red Lips sprints fast up the ramp.

As he storms snorting
onto the platform, I look down
at the empty stands. I wave
my hand, pretending to be famous.
Red Lips bends his head,
tilting down, and Arnette
leans forward. "Ready?" she says.
"You're now the girl
on the high-diving horse."

Red Lips jumps,
and it's like flying:
wind in my hair
and sunshine in my eyes.
I cry out,
squealing and shouting,
as we fall
down,
down,
down,
sloshing into the tank.

The water is cold;
I tremble and shiver
and swim to the side,
Red Lips smiling close behind.
Papa stands at the side,
his smile wide with pride,
clicking lots of pictures.

Ten years later, at the age
of eighteen, sea breeze once again
tickles my eyes when I arrive
in Atlantic City. It's the summer
of 1946, and Ivy Cordelia from
Philadelphia has come to stay:
The Girl on the High-Diving Horse.
Papa takes lots of pictures.

AUTHOR'S NOTE

My family visited the Steel Pier in the '60s and '70s, and I was fascinated by the diving horses. It was an incredible sight to a child: A majestic horse silhouetted high in the summer-blue sky. The horse would pause for one suspenseful and dramatic moment . . . and then . . . splash! The vision of the horse flying through the sky stayed with me even when I closed my eyes at night. Atlantic City truly was a magical place in earlier days, and its sights and sounds and smells remain with me to this day.

In researching the book, I visited Arnette French, a lady in her eighties who'd been a diving-horse girl many years ago. Arnette was a most graceful and cordial woman, and she was thrilled at the idea of this book. She had many fond memories of her high-diving horse days, and she relayed story after story of horses who loved to dive. Her sister, Sonora Carver, was also a diving-horse girl; she now lives in a nursing home in New Jersey, where she still dreams of her days as "The Girl on the High-Diving Horse." Sadly, Arnette has passed on.

Years ago, when I first met the illustrator Ted Lewin, I mentioned that I'd always wanted to write about the high-diving horses of Atlantic City. Ted responded that he'd always wanted to illustrate such a book, and I'm thankful that he has done so . . . beautifully.

My gratitude is extended to Allen "Boo" Pergament, curator of the most exquisite collection of Atlantic City memorabilia in New Jersey, who most kindly allowed Ted and me to choose any and all prints that we needed for this book.

Thanks to Christine Means (my son Justin's "Girl") for modeling as The Girl on the High-Diving Horse.

ILLUSTRATOR'S NOTE

To capture the feel of the period, I've made my illustrations in the style of linen postcards that were very popular in the 1930s and '40s. Linen postcards were not really linen. The picture side had a woven, linenlike texture. Five colors were printed over a black-and-white photographic image. The cards depicted, with great spirit and optimism, every main street, storefront, gas station and tourist destination. Their gaudy colors and photo retouching gave the cards a fantasy look. Everything looked better than it was. To re-create the look, I first made a black-and-white painting, then applied thin washes using a limited number of colors.

Illustrating this book was a nostalgic journey for me. When I was a child, my whole family vacationed in Atlantic City for two weeks every summer. We always stayed in the New Belmont Hotel on the boardwalk in room 401, the same room my father used to stay in with his parents. My kid brother and I spent many happy days strolling on the boardwalk and exploring the Steel Pier. We saw the wild animal acts, the trapeze artists and the high-diving horses, "All for one general admission!"

PATRICIA LEE GAUCH, EDITOR

PHILOMEL BOOKS,
a division of Penguin Putnam Books for Young Readers,
345 Hudson Street, New York, NY 10014.
Philomel Books, Reg. U.S. Pat. & Tm. Off. Published simultaneously in Canada.
Manufactured in China by South China Printing Co. (1988) Ltd.

Book design by Semadar Megged.
The text is set in 19-point Rosabel Antique.

Library of Congress Cataloging-in-Publication Data
High, Linda Oatman.
The girl on the high-diving horse / by Linda Oatman High : illustrated by Ted Lewin. p. cm.
Summary: Eight-year-old Ivy Cordelia spends the summer of 1936 in Atlantic City with her
photographer father, and dreams of being the girl who perches on a horse as it dives into a tank of
water.   [1. Stunt performers–Fiction. 2. Amusement parks–Fiction. 3. Horses–Fiction. 4. Atlantic
City (N.J.)–Fiction.]   I. Lewin, Ted, ill. II. Title.   PZ7.H543968 Gi 2003   [Fic]–dc21   2001036441
ISBN 0-399-23649-X
10 9 8 7 6 5 4 3 2 1
First Impression